For my own little vacuum lover. Always remember: it is okay to love the peculiar - it keeps things interesting and colorful.

Published by LHCpublishing 2015

The Impatient Little Vacuum
Text Copyright © 2015 Yvonne Jones
Illustrations Copyright © 2015 Yvonne Jones

Printed in the USA.

All rights reserved.
No part of this book may be
reproduced in any form
without the written permission
of the copyright holder.

All inquiries should be directed to
www.LHCpublishing.com

ISBN-13: 978-0-69247-443-3
ISBN-10: 0-69247-443-9

PUBLISHING

The impatient little Vacuum

written by
YVONNE JONES

Did you know that late at night, when all the people are asleep, toys and appliances and machines and anything that usually doesn't move during the day comes to life? It's true! And really quite interesting. Interesting, because so many wonderful and exciting stories happen during these magical hours.

One such story takes place right here, in this old fashioned Mom and Pop store located where Main Street and Piper Avenue meet.

It just so happened that Mom and Pop, who owned this store, had a whole aisle full of vacuum cleaners. No two vacuums looked alike. They were all different models and created for different purposes.

"VROOM - VROOM! Out of my way!" The droning sound came from DIRK MEVIL, the loudest and bravest vacuum in the whole entire store. "Watch out! Watch out! Im coming!" If there was one thing that DIRK MEVIL loved to do, it was racing the other vacuums. All the time! So much so, that the others started to get tired of his constant dashing and whizzing.

"Give me a break!" said LISSELL, the girliest vacuum of them all. She loved her pink and shiny coat and was always worried about getting her hose and brushes dirty. "If you keep on whirring around like this, you'll wake up the shop owners. Besides, I need my beauty sleep, so I look nice and fresh in the morning. I'm sure tomorrow will be the day when people will come to buy me for their home!"

That was what all the vacuums wanted: to be purchased and taken to a forever-home.

"But you just got here last week!" said CORIK, the smartest and most intelligent vacuum that you could ever imagine. He learned his A-B-Cs and his 1-2-3s before he even knew how to properly suck up dirt through his hose.

"I know I haven't been here long," replied LISSELL. "But I really do believe that tomorrow might be my day!"

"Are you sure that you even want to be picked?" asked RHARK. RHARK was the silly one in this aisle. "You do realize that you will have to get dirty eventually, right? After all, you ARE a vacuum cleaner!"

"Well," answered LISSELL, "I'm planning on sucking up clean dirt only! And I also expect to get my filter cleaned after every use. That's how I perform best!"

10

"Good luck finding a forever-home with all these crazy wishes," chuckled BENMORE, the strongest and mightiest of the bunch. He was extremely flexible and very quick to pick up any dirt he could find. His strong build showed strength and durability. "Most of us will be lucky to get our dust canisters and brushes and filters cleaned once or twice a year!"

"And have you ever heard of clean dirt?" snorted RHARK. "What does THAT look like anyway?"

"Fluffy, and pink, and glittery of course!" replied LISSELL. "I cannot wait to have my canister filled with shiny tinsel and glittery confetti!"

"Shiny tinsel and glittery confetti?" laughed RHARK. "More like smelly lentil and sticky spaghetti!"

The others giggled.

"Oh yeah? Just you wait and see!" blurted LISSELL. "I WILL find my perfect forever-home!" And with that, she spun around and rolled away.

RHARK and BENMORE both chuckled. This LISSELL sure had a loose belt!

MYSON, a little boy vacuum, chimed in. "If someone is going to get picked, it's LISSELL. She is shiny, and beautiful, and the newest model of her brand." He sadly let his brushes hang. MYSON had been in this store for almost two whole weeks already, but had not been picked by any of the customers. He was really starting to worry. "I have been here for 13 days now! I don't think I'll ever find a forever-home!"

He worried, because he really did look quite different from all the other vacuums. The colors of his frame were intensely bright, and this ball-like shape on his lower end... Well, it just didn't look right to him. No other vacuum had such a clumsy-looking thing. What was it meant to do anyway? MYSON was truly concerned.

14

"Now, now, my dear." A calming voice made its way toward the front of the store. "Don't you worry, MYSON! Everything has its time and place. You have to be patient, that's all!" The kind words came from MRS. DOOVER, the oldest and wisest vacuum of them all. She was Mom & Pop's personal vacuum cleaner that made sure the place was spic and span and dust-free after the store closed every night. She was not the newest kind (quite old, really), but she sure knew how to take care of all the other little vacuums that waited to be picked out by one of the customers.

"I think you look really nice, MYSON," shy SUREKA said. "I especially like your bright colors! They are very beautiful!" SUREKA was a humble little vacuum. Her mother, SELECTROBLUX, taught her that kindness is one of the most important qualities of a hardworking vacuum cleaner.

"See?" said MRS. DOOVER. "What seems mismatched and different to you is quite interesting to others. Besides, do we really want to all look the same? I think this would make this place much less special, don't you?"

Of course MRS. DOOVER was right. Not everyone can look or think or feel the same! And that is quite alright! With that, the little vacuums yawned a big yawn, rolled up their power cords, and put themselves onto their shelves again to have a restful night.

The next morning was greeted with a cheerful and noisy clanging of the front store door bell. Mom and Pop opened their little store bright and early every morning. Usually, customers didn't start to show up until at least noon. But today, unexpectedly, a very cheerful lady walked through the door right after it had been unlocked.

"Excuse me," she said, "I'm looking for a vacuum cleaner."

These were the words all vacuums were waiting to hear. Immediately, they straightened themselves, pushing out their handles so as to appear taller than they really were. One of them was going to find a forever-home today. But who would it be?

"How about this pink one over here? Yes, that one! My girls will just love it!" LISSELL couldn't believe her luck! She had been right: she did find an owner today. LISSELL happily winked at the others with her dirt sensor light before she was safely wrapped and packed up in her box.

And so it continued for the rest of the week. Two more vacuums were sold. MUG MOCTOR, a deep cleaning vacuum with a huge water tank, found a home with a cleaning company. And PALALODIC, a friendly little girl vacuum, was purchased by an elderly couple who wanted something lighter and easier to clean their carpets with. Their old one had become too heavy for them to push around, so they were very happy about their new little cleaner.

22

While MYSON was really happy for LISSELL, MUG MOCTOR and PALALODIC, he started to worry again. What if all the others would get sold? What if he would be the only one left behind? Whom would he talk to? What would he do by himself?

"I don't think I want to be a vacuum cleaner anymore," MYSON said. "I don't even know how to clean. I mean... not really. I have never tried to suck up any dirt before. What if I can't do it?"

"Don't you worry," replied CORIK, while adjusting his glasses. "I know you can do it. It's really quite simple. We basically work like a straw that little boys and girls drink their juice with. But we have a motor, and we suck up dirt and dust instead of juice. The sucked up

23

dirt gets collected in our bags or canisters, and filters prevent the dust from going into our motors in case it gets out of the bags."

CORIK smiled at MYSON. He was proud of how much he knew, and he was more than happy to share it with his friends. "Of course we need electricity to do all that. That's why we all have power cords."

A vacuum cleaner works like a straw? "Well, I can do that," replied MYSON relieved. "Thank you, CORIK, for trying to make me feel better! You are a good friend!"

"Yes, he is!" said MRS. DOOVER from the corner tucked in beside the counter, where Mom had left her after a quick vacuum of the dirt on a young man's boots earlier. "And he is right, MYSON! You CAN do it! You just have to believe in yourself."

MYSON felt much better. What wonderful friends he had. He was glad he had someone to talk to and to share his worries with. Of course he could do it! That's what he was made for after all, right? And with that, he closed his eyes and fell asleep.

That evening, MYSON was awakened by loud vrooming and revving noises right there, somewhere in the shop. What was going on? He opened his sleepy eyes. DIRK MEVIL and BENMORE were standing right next to each other, each with a line of dirt spread out before them. Dust bunnies, lost coins, crumbs, dirt from muddy shoes - they used anything they could find.

"Ladies and gentlevacs," RHARK announced excitedly. "Get ready for the competition of your life! Whoever races down the aisle first while sucking up *all* the dirt will be our winner. Get your wheels ready, your nozzles set, and... GO!"

A loud hum of air started off the race. Every vacuum standing along the side was cheering. Noisy rattling sounds of solid things being sucked into the nozzles filled the air. What a race!

DIRK MEVIL swerved down the aisle. BENMORE followed closely behind, trying to take the lead. Leaving some crumbs of dirt on the floor, DIRK MEVIL accelerated and crossed RHARK's power cord that made up the finish line at the end of the shelves.

"I won! I won!" shouted DIRK MEVIL happily, spinning in a circle on his wheels. "I am the fastest!" He loved to race, and he *loved* to win.

"You sure were the fastest," responded MRS. DOOVER, while approaching slowly on her small and squeaky wheels. "But sometimes, speed isn't all that matters. Look how much dirt you left behind. BENMORE sucked up all the dirt on his side of the aisle. I guess for today, you will have to share the victory."

When DIRK MEVIL saw the mess he had left behind, he had to admit that he hadn't given his best in the race. He knew that he could have done better. And because he was a good sportsman, he shook BENMORE's handle graciously and promised to do a better job next time. He would show off his speed AND do a fantastic job sucking up all the dirt on the way to victory.

Three more vacuums were sold that week. CORIK was picked by a friendly-looking janitor of a local school. This was just perfect for CORIK. He was very excited because taking care of a school meant that he would be able to learn even more after he was done with all his work every day. He was sure to become the smartest little vacuum cleaner the world had ever seen.

DIRK MEVIL was purchased by the owner of a car shop that specialized in repairing old-fashioned sports cars. He couldn't have been happier. Now he would be able to refine his racing skills by learning from the best.

And the third vacuum that found a home that week was kind, little SUREKA. A hairstylist had chosen SUREKA for her salon, a bright and busy place for a little vacuum.

It was beginning to get really quiet on Mom & Pops vacuum shelf. And a bit lonely. At least MYSON felt this way.

Easily bored, RHARK asked MYSON, "What should we do tonight?" as he looked around the bare shelves.

"Maybe we could play some Swivel-Ball," answered BENMORE, nudging a ball he had found in aisle 4 toward his friends. "What about you, MYSON? Do you want to join us?"

"No thanks," responded MYSON, as he nervously chewed on his belt. He was too worried to play anything right now. He desperately wanted a forever-home. 'Only three of us left,' he thought.

'What am I going to do?'

MRS. DOOVER knew the expression on his face. She had seen it many times before. She called it the *troubled face*. One of the last vacuum cleaners always ended up with a *troubled face*, out of fear not to be chosen for a forever-home.

"Remember what I told you," she said to MYSON. "Everything has its time and place. You will find a lovely family eventually. Until then, practice patience, my little one."

With that, she rolled off, settling into her corner next to the broom and dustpan.

Was it really the end of the week already? MYSON couldn't believe it. The sun was brightly shining through the store window, and the birds happily chirped their lovely songs.

"What a beautiful day," MYSON thought. He even caught himself whistling quietly along with the tune of the birds.

The loud clanging of the store's front door pulled him out of his daydream. A charming woman and her little boy entered. The wide-eyed boy seemed very excited.

"Mommy, mommy! There they are!" he said, pointing toward the back of the store. Tugging on her arm, he pulled her toward the shelves.

"I'm coming, I'm coming!" his mother said with a big smile on her face. This was the day her little boy had been waiting for. For such a long time! She wasn't quite sure why, but he just LOVED vacuum cleaners. He knew every single brand by heart, had her read to him everything they could find about vacuums, and talked about them all the time.

"I can't believe we're finally going to pick one today! Which one should we get, mommy? Which one?" the little boy asked. "I like this one right here. It looks exactly like the one in my book. Look at its perfect shape and how bright it is! And look, it has room for two whole liters of dirt and dust inside! And so many extra tools! I'm sure this one will do a great job. Please, mommy! Can we pick this one?"

MYSON couldn't believe it. Was this little boy really pointing at him? He'd never seen anyone so excited and happy about picking a vacuum cleaner. This must be a very special little boy. All of a sudden, MYSON felt very proud. He stuck out his canister, straightened his handle, and aligned his ball-like shape on his lower end to make extra sure that the boy saw all his wonderful and special features.

"This one it is, then," the boy's mother said, as she took her son by the hand, and led him toward the front of the store to pay for their new vacuum cleaner.

"Can you believe this?" MYSON whispered to MRS. DOOVER, who was propped by his shelf where Pop had left her. "This little boy picked me! ME!" MYSON was so happy that a tiny little tear rolled down along the side of his canister. He had been waiting for this moment for such a long time. He couldn't believe his luck. All his patience had finally paid off. He found a forever-home with a boy that not only seemed to really love vacuums, but that truly appreciated every single part about his build.

While MYSON's new owner paid, MRS. DOOVER gently wrapped her hose around MYSON's canister in a hug. "This little boy accepts you for who you are. He values your special features and unique look. See, MYSON?

Being different IS okay. At times, this might be hard to remember, but always celebrate the way you are." She gave him another little squeeze. And then, MYSON was lifted out of the shelf and put into a box that would get him safely to his new forever-home.

The End.

The artwork that inspired

The impatient little vacuum

Bissell   Turbo Cat   Kenmore   Shark

by CKJ - 4 years old

OTHER WORKS BY THIS AUTHOR

SAFETY GOOSE
CHILDREN'S SAFETY – ONE RHYME
AT A TIME

NOW I SEE: ANIMALS
HIGH CONTRAST BOOK FOR BABIES

TEENY TOTTY™ USES MAMA'S BIG POTTY
TRANSITION FROM POTTY CHAIR TO
TOILET

NOW I SEE: TOYS
HIGH CONTRAST BOOK FOR BABIES

GOT GARBAGE? – THE GARBAGE BOOK
FOR THE BIGGEST GARBAGE FAN

CLOSING THE GAP – UNDERSTANDING YOUR
SERVICE (WO)MAN

37740751R00029

Made in the USA
Middletown, DE
06 December 2016